Some things are
sometimes red...

Some things are
usually red...

Some things are
almost always red.

What red things do you see?

DK

A DK PUBLISHING BOOK

Published in the United States by DK Publishing, Inc.,
95 Madison Avenue, New York, New York 10016
Copyright © 1993 Dorling Kindersley Limited, London
All rights reserved   ISBN 1-56458-313-9
Color reproduction by Colourscan, Singapore
Printed in Singapore by Tien Wah Press Ltd

Red

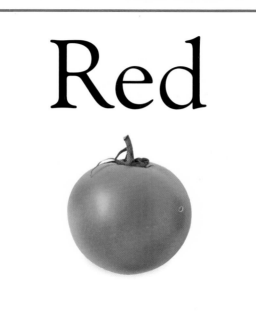

strawberries

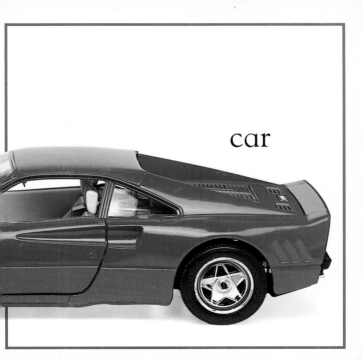

car

rose

soap

ladybug

boot

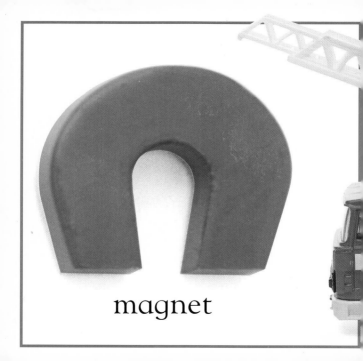

magnet

fire truck

telephone

raspberries

boxing
glove

chilies

tomatoes

shirt

parrot

apple